USBORNE
Le

USBORNE FIRST READING
Snails
Susanna Davidson
Illustrated by Rocío Martínez

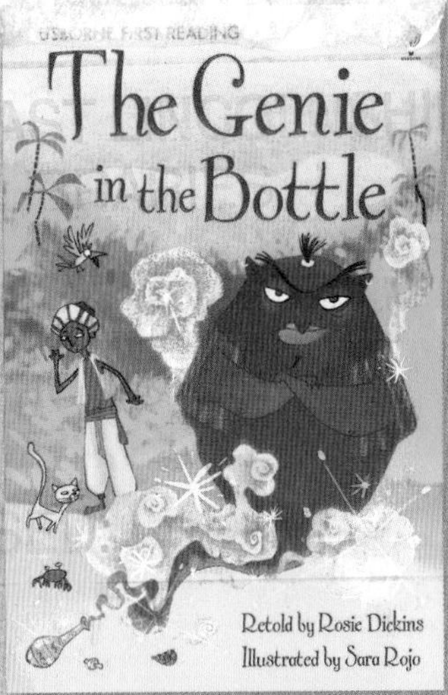
USBORNE FIRST READING
The Genie in the Bottle
Retold by Rosie Dickins
Illustrated by Sara Rojo

USBORNE FIRST READING
THE STONECUTTER
RETOLD BY LYNNE BENTON
ILLUSTRATED BY LEE COSGROVE

USBORNE FIRST READING
There Was A Crooked Man

The Daydreamer

Retold by Kate Davies

Illustrated by Kate Sheppard

Reading consultant: Alison Kelly
Roehampton University

Daisy has no money.
"Take my milk
to market," says
the farmer.

I'll give you a gold coin.

"Yes!" says Daisy.

And she sets off for the market.

“Soon I’ll have some money,” she thinks.

I can buy a hen.

My hen will lay eggs...

...lots of eggs.

I can sell my eggs.

I'll have lots of money!

I'll buy a pretty dress...

...and sparkly shoes.

But I won't get dressed by myself.

I'll have servants to help me!

I'll marry a prince.

I'll be a princess.

We'll live in
a palace...

...with golden gates.

We'll have a ball.

I'll twirl and whirl in my new dress.

SPLISH!
SPLASH!
SPLOSH!

The milk is gone!
Poor Daisy.

PUZZLES

Puzzle 1

Can you spot the differences between the two pictures?

There are
six to find.

Puzzle 2
Match the words to the picture.

palace

pony

prince

Daisy

dogs

hill

hen

Puzzle 3

Choose the best speech bubble for each picture.

We're dancing.
We're swimming.

I can buy a hen.
I can buy a banana.
Cheese
Hens = 1 gold co

Answers to puzzles

Puzzle 1

Puzzle 2

Puzzle 3

"There are lots of eggs!"

"We're dancing."

"I can buy a hen."

About The Daydreamer

The Daydreamer is one of Aesop's Fables, a collection of stories first told in Ancient Greece. Today, different versions of the story are told all around the world. In India, the daydreamer is a poor man who dreams of selling his last bowl of food. In Russia, the daydreamer is a thief who dreams of selling stolen cucumbers.

Designed by Lisa Verrall
Series editor: Lesley Sims
Series designer: Russell Punter

First published in 2010 by Usborne Publishing Ltd., Usborne House, 83-85 Saffron Hill, London EC1N 8RT, England. www.usborne.com

UE. First published in America in 2010.

USBORNE FIRST READING
Level Three

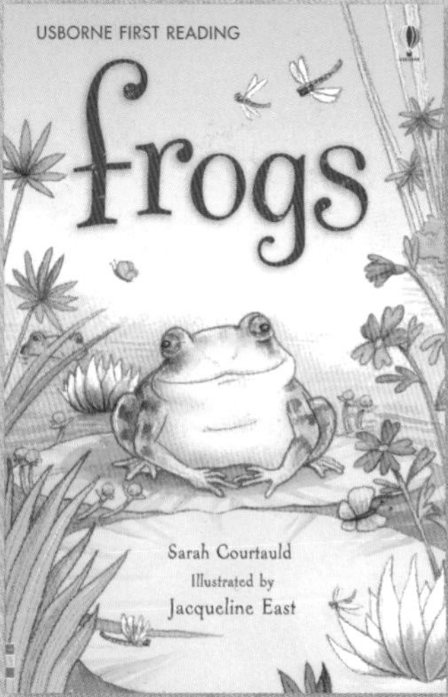